W9-BFK-270

retold by J. Patrick Lewis

# THE FROG PRINCESS
· A RUSSIAN FOLKTALE ·

paintings by Gennady Spirin

*Dial Books*

New York

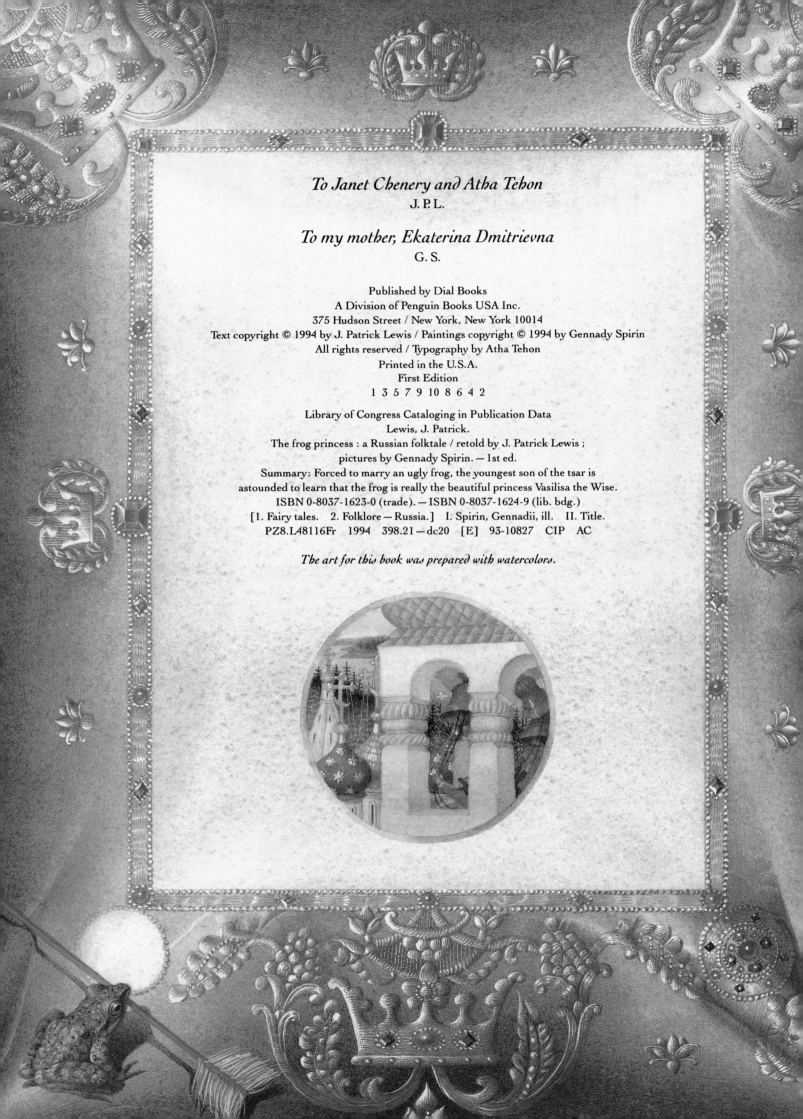

*To Janet Chenery and Atha Tehon*
J. P. L.

*To my mother, Ekaterina Dmitrievna*
G. S.

Published by Dial Books
A Division of Penguin Books USA Inc.
375 Hudson Street / New York, New York 10014
Text copyright © 1994 by J. Patrick Lewis / Paintings copyright © 1994 by Gennady Spirin
All rights reserved / Typography by Atha Tehon
Printed in the U.S.A.
First Edition
1 3 5 7 9 10 8 6 4 2

Library of Congress Cataloging in Publication Data
Lewis, J. Patrick.
The frog princess : a Russian folktale / retold by J. Patrick Lewis ;
pictures by Gennady Spirin. — 1st ed.
Summary: Forced to marry an ugly frog, the youngest son of the tsar is
astounded to learn that the frog is really the beautiful princess Vasilisa the Wise.
ISBN 0-8037-1623-0 (trade). — ISBN 0-8037-1624-9 (lib. bdg.)
[1. Fairy tales.   2. Folklore — Russia.]   I. Spirin, Gennadii, ill.   II. Title.
PZ8.L48116Fr   1994   398.21 — dc20   [E]   93-10827   CIP   AC

*The art for this book was prepared with watercolors.*

Once long ago in a faraway kingdom there lived a great tsar who had three sons. When it came time for them to marry, the tsar called the princes to his side and said, "String your bows with the strength of ten men, and shoot an arrow as far as you can into the heart of Russia. Whoever finds your arrow shall be your bride."

3

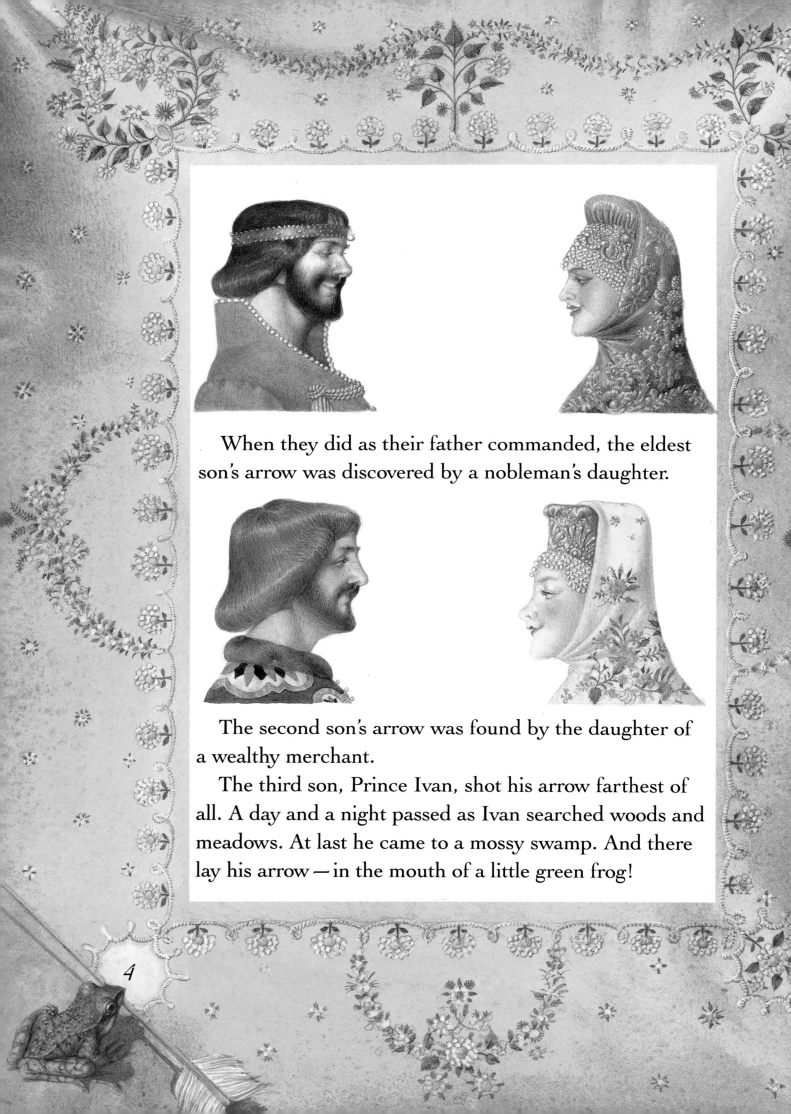

When they did as their father commanded, the eldest son's arrow was discovered by a nobleman's daughter.

The second son's arrow was found by the daughter of a wealthy merchant.

The third son, Prince Ivan, shot his arrow farthest of all. A day and a night passed as Ivan searched woods and meadows. At last he came to a mossy swamp. And there lay his arrow — in the mouth of a little green frog!

4

Prince Ivan wept bitterly at the sight of her. "How can I marry *you*?" he cried.

"If that is your fate, dear prince," the frog croaked, "then make me your bride."

The young prince remembered his father's command. Sadly he put the frog in his pocket and returned home.

When his brothers saw Ivan's bride-to-be, they laughed and laughed. But the very next day the weddings were held in the Grand Palace, and the three princes married the two maidens…and a frog carried on a silver platter by the Imperial Guards!

After the wedding feast the tsar wondered which of his daughters-in-law was the cleverest. So he said to his sons, "Tell your wives to weave me the finest robe in the land!"

Well, you can imagine Ivan's despair. That night he told his wife about the tsar's command. "A frog can't stitch a button on a sleeve much less sew a fine robe! What am I to do?"

"Sleep well, Prince Ivan," croaked the frog. "Morning brings its own surprise."

As soon as the young prince had gone off to bed, the frog gently removed her skin. Instantly she appeared as Vasilisa the Wise, a radiantly beautiful princess! Throwing open the window, she sang to the wind: "Come to me, Night Maidens, and weave a tsar's robe like no other."

And so it was done. Before Ivan awoke the next morning, the Night Maidens had returned with their treasure. His frog wife perched herself on the elegant sleeve of a velvet robe, ringed with rubies and emeralds. Ivan was so overjoyed that he ran to show the robe to his father.

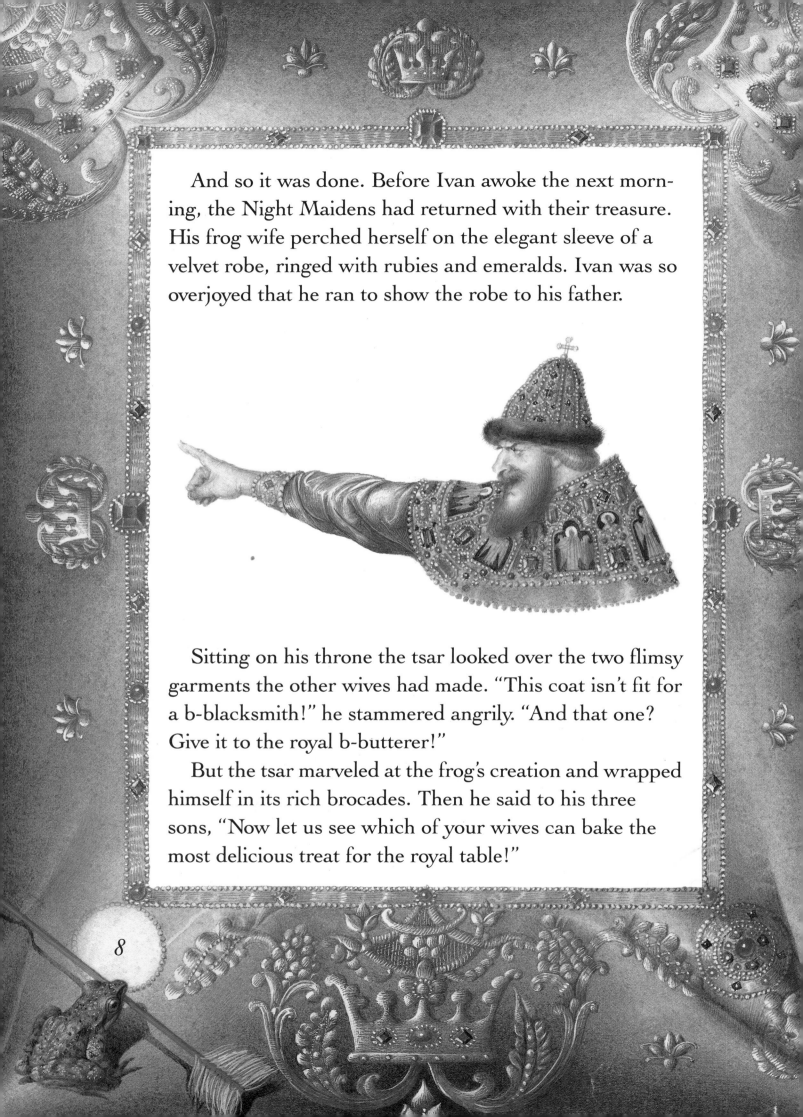

Sitting on his throne the tsar looked over the two flimsy garments the other wives had made. "This coat isn't fit for a b-blacksmith!" he stammered angrily. "And that one? Give it to the royal b-butterer!"

But the tsar marveled at the frog's creation and wrapped himself in its rich brocades. Then he said to his three sons, "Now let us see which of your wives can bake the most delicious treat for the royal table!"

The young prince pitied himself the whole day through. When night fell, he trudged back to his chambers. "What is it, Prince Ivan?" the frog wife asked. "Is the tsar displeased with my gift?"

"A frog can't bake a tart," Ivan wept, "much less a treat fit for royalty!"

"Sleep well, dear prince," said the frog. "Morning brings its own surprise."

Again he went off to bed. And again the frog climbed out of her frog self…and into Vasilisa the Wise! She flew to the window, singing to the wind: "Night Maidens, if you please, bake a delicacy fit for His Majesty!"

The next morning the frog was sitting there beside an enormous cake. Overcome with joy, Prince Ivan ordered the guards to take it to the palace at once. There on the throne the angry tsar glared at his elder sons' wives. Royal treats indeed! A lumpy tart, oozing pudding all over the carpet! A ginger cookie that nearly chipped his tooth!

"Enough!" bellowed the tsar. "Can no one bake a royal treat?!"

Just then the frog's creation was carried in. The entire court gasped! A wedding cake in the shape of the Grand Palace itself, glittering with candied domes and sugar spires. The tsar happily called to his three sons and said, "A royal pastry calls for a royal feast. Tonight we will have

a Grand Ball. And Ivan, don't forget to bring your little green bride."

Prince Ivan returned to his frog wife, hung his head in shame, and told her about the feast to come. "A frog can't even curtsy much less dance! What am I to do?"

"Have no fear, prince," said the frog. "Go to the ball alone. When lightning flashes, tell the guests, 'My frog wife has arrived.'"

That evening Prince Ivan had no sooner entered the palace, bustling with hundreds of guests, than his brothers began laughing. "Well now, Ivan, where is your little green wife? Have you left her at home to charm the lily pads?"

11

Moments later a lightning bolt creased the night sky. Embarrassed, but gathering all his courage, Prince Ivan stepped forward and spoke: "My frog wife has arrived."

A royal coach and six white horses clattered into the cobblestone courtyard! The guests gaped out the windows as a beautiful woman—it was Vasilisa the Wise!—stepped from her carriage. Her hair was the color of the sun, her eyes the color of the sea, and her dazzling gown was adorned with pearls.

Followed by the Night Maidens, she swept into the Great Hall and took her astonished husband by the hand as the guests stared in amazement. Envy seized the wives of the two elder brothers. They watched Vasilisa closely, and secretly vowed to imitate everything she did.

At the splendid banquet table, the guests ate, drank, and made merry. Vasilisa dined on roast swan and daintily tucked the bones up her right sleeve. She sipped the wine, then poured a few drops on her left sleeve. The two sly wives did likewise.

When Prince Ivan and Vasilisa the Wise began to dance, she waved her left arm gracefully. From the wine drops a shimmering lake appeared—right there in the middle of the Grand Ballroom. Then she waved her right arm—and from the tiny bones a flock of magnificent swans settled on the water.

Not to be outdone, the two wives flailed their arms wildly. But the wine from their sleeves splattered the guests. The bones flew out and smacked the tsar on his royal chin! In a rage he ordered them out of the banquet hall.

Delighted with his third daughter-in-law, the tsar bowed to the charming Frog Princess, and asked her to dance. As they did so, the prince slipped out of the palace and ran as fast as he could back to his chambers. He could not believe that his homely frog and his beautiful wife were one and the same.

There on the floor next to his bed lay a shriveled green frog skin. Ah, if I burn it, Prince Ivan thought, she will remain a beautiful woman forever! So into the fire it went.

Later that night Vasilisa returned home and found her skin turned to ashes. "Oh, dear prince, what have you done?" she cried. "If only you could have waited three more days. Now I am lost to you forever—unless you can find me in a Kingdom beyond Blue Kingdoms!"

And in the blink of an eye Vasilisa the Wise turned into a swan, leaped to the window ledge, and vanished.

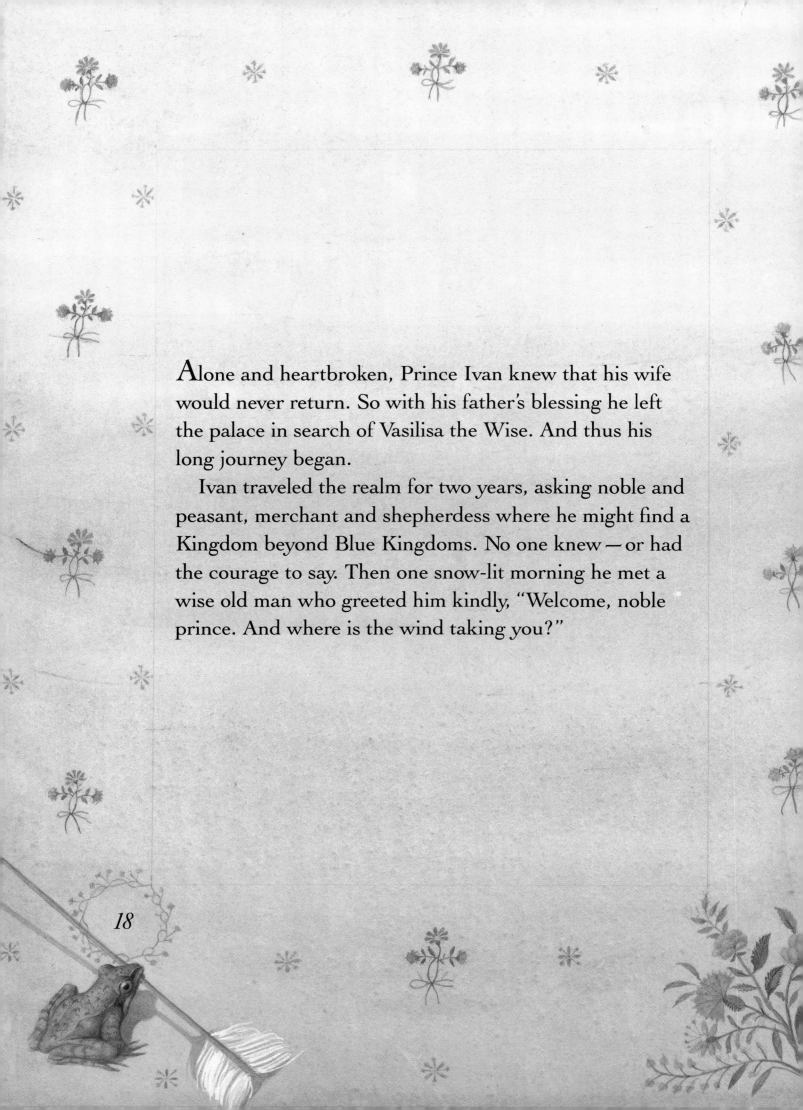

Alone and heartbroken, Prince Ivan knew that his wife would never return. So with his father's blessing he left the palace in search of Vasilisa the Wise. And thus his long journey began.

Ivan traveled the realm for two years, asking noble and peasant, merchant and shepherdess where he might find a Kingdom beyond Blue Kingdoms. No one knew — or had the courage to say. Then one snow-lit morning he met a wise old man who greeted him kindly, "Welcome, noble prince. And where is the wind taking you?"

Ivan told him all that had happened — the sad tale of a frog who was a princess.

"Oh, Prince Ivan," the old man said, "what possessed you to burn that frog skin? It was not yours to take. Vasilisa the Wise is an enchanted princess, and because she was born much cleverer than her father, he condemned her to live for three years as a frog. But you destroyed her skin three days before the evil spell would have ended.

"Here," the old man continued, "take this ball of yarn. Throw it as far as you can, and follow wherever it leads you. As the yarn unwinds, so too will your fate."

The prince thanked him for his advice, puzzling as it was. He threw the ball of yarn deep into an ancient forest, and set off to find it. In the winter-white woods, among gnarled trees aching with ice, he suddenly found himself face to face with a bear! Prince Ivan readied his bow and took aim. But just as he was about to loose his arrow, the bear pleaded, "Spare me, Prince Ivan. The day is not far off when I can help you."

So the prince put down his bow, watched the bear shuffle away through the snow, and threw the ball of yarn even farther. By midday Ivan saw a falcon flying overhead. An hour later, by the shore of a deep blue lake he spotted an enormous pike. Very tasty indeed, thought Ivan.

He had taken out his bow and arrow to catch his dinner, but he shot neither the falcon nor the very tasty pike, for they had said exactly the same thing as the bear: "Spare me, Prince Ivan. The day is not far off when I can help you."

Now the sun rode swiftly down the sky, and night was huddled in the trees. Ivan, hungry and tired, threw the yarn once more. On and on it rolled through yet another forest, stopping in front of a strange cottage that spun around on chicken feet!

The young prince shouted:

> *Little hut, little hut,*
> *Stand the old way as thy mother stood thee,*
> *With thy back to the woods and thy front to me!*

At once the hut stood still.

Ivan went to the doorway, and standing there was Baba Yaga, the Wicked Nasty! A witch, a hag, a crone. Take your pick — she was three in one. And until now no one had dared come near her.

"What do you want with me?" Baba Yaga demanded.

"First, prepare a bath and a bite to eat, granny," the prince replied. "Then I'll tell you my story."

Taken back by Prince Ivan's boldness, Baba Yaga took him in, fed him toadstool broth and cackleberry tea, and listened to his tale of woe. Then she said, "Your frog wife is a prisoner in the Kingdom beyond Blue Kingdoms, in the castle of Koshchei the Invincible.

"Unless you slay him," she continued, "you will never see Vasilisa again. Koshchei is mightier than ten legions—and too wicked times three!

"Listen to me, Prince Ivan: His fate lies in the tip of a needle,

a needle that is in an egg.

The egg is inside a duck,

and the duck is inside a wild hare.

Not far from Koshchei's castle, the hare sleeps
in a golden cage,

nestled in the branches of a tall oak tree.

If you succeed where all others have failed, you will
have your reward!"

The next morning Prince Ivan left Baba Yaga's and set out for the Kingdom beyond Blue Kingdoms. It was late in the day when he arrived at the foot of the oak tree…so tall that its top was lost in the clouds. There on a high branch out of reach lay the golden cage. Ivan waited for nightfall, when he knew Koshchei would be sleeping. Then he shook the tree with all his might. Not a single leaf fluttered.

Suddenly the bear whose life Prince Ivan had spared appeared out of nowhere. He wrapped his huge paws around the oak tree, pulling it up by its roots.

28

When the cage crashed to the ground and split open, the wild hare landed on a bramble bush and was torn to pieces. And out of its belly flew a duck.

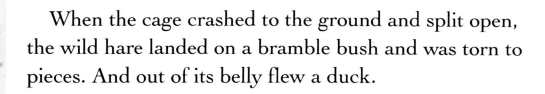

Instantly the falcon whose life Ivan had spared chased the duck through the sky. Ivan ran after them until he reached a clearing that opened onto a deep blue lake. Overhead the duck, frightened by the screaming falcon, dropped her egg in the water. It sank to the bottom like a stone.

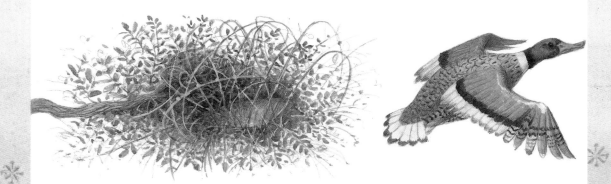

Ivan sat down at the far end of sadness. Even the waves grieved with him. The egg and the needle were lost for good, and so now was his beloved Vasilisa.

But soon there came another sound. The pike whose life Ivan had spared leaped up at the water's edge — with the precious egg in his jaws! Ivan waded into the shallow water, fetched the egg, cracked it open, and found the needle just as Baba Yaga had foretold. He bent the tip until it snapped off....*Aiiieee!*

At that instant the air was filled with the mournful cry of Koshchei, dying, invincible no more.

Prince Ivan ran back to the evil castle. There Vasilisa the Wise, even more beautiful than before, threw herself in his arms. "My father's curse is broken, Prince Ivan. I am your bride forever."

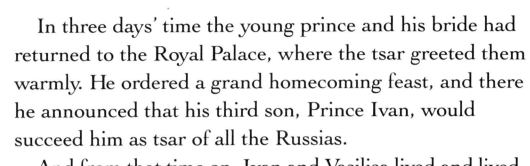

In three days' time the young prince and his bride had returned to the Royal Palace, where the tsar greeted them warmly. He ordered a grand homecoming feast, and there he announced that his third son, Prince Ivan, would succeed him as tsar of all the Russias.

And from that time on, Ivan and Vasilisa lived and lived, and they barred the door against misfortune.